W9-CYA-888

The Tempest

ABOUT THE AUTHOR

Beverley Birch grew up in Kenya and first came to England, where she now lives with her husband and two daughters, at the age of fifteen. After completing an MA in Economics and Sociology, Beverley became an editor at Penguin. Within a few weeks she was offered the chance to work on children's books and has been involved in children's publishing – as both editor and writer – ever since.

She has had over forty books published, from picture books and novels to science biographies and retellings of classic works. All her titles have received critical acclaim and her work has been translated into more than a dozen languages. Her latest novel for teenagers, *Rift*, was published in 2006.

Shakespeare's Tales

The Tempest

Retold by Beverley Birch

Illustrated by Peter Chesterton

WAYLAND

For my mother, with love

Text copyright © 2002 Beverley Birch
Illustrations copyright © 2006 Peter Chesterton

First published in *Shakespeare's Tales* in 2002 by
Hodder Children's Books
This edition first published in 2006 by
Wayland, an imprint of Hachette Children's Books

Cover and text design: Rosamund Saunders

Hachette Children's Books
338 Euston Road, London NW1 3BH

Printed and bound in the United Kingdom

ISBN-10: 0 7502 4961 7
ISBN-13: 978 0 7502 4961 4

The Cast

Prospero – rightful Duke of Milan

Miranda – Prospero's daughter

Ariel – Prospero's spirit servant

Caliban – savage native of the island

THE SHIPWRECK VICTIMS

Alonso – King of Naples

Ferdinand – son and heir to Alonso

Antonio – Prospero's brother

Gonzalo – trusted Lord of Prospero

Sebastian – Alonso's brother

Trinculo – jester

Stephano – drunken butler

I t was the frenzy of a raging animal, the fury of wind and sea that seized the ship. Thunder like the crack of doom; the flare of lightning across the decks. Flames engulfed the mast, a blazing furnace belched forth sailors wrestling with their burning vessel and its shrieking cargo: a king, a prince, a duke and lords.

But what did a royal cargo matter to that fury of wind and sea? Could a king's command throw back those mountainous waves? Could a lord's great wealth buy life or death before that tempest? There were no great or small, no rich or poor – only men, who shrieked before the

thunder's power and knew their end
had come.

The ship burned like a funeral pyre,
split, was engulfed in a final, savage swell,
and sank.

The watchers, high on a rocky
headland, gazed in silence. Nothing but
scattered splinters on a foaming sea. The
one, a girl, stood pale, her huddled body
speaking misery at each pitiful cry of
helpless men.

Her companion stood, unmoving.
There was no trace of pity, joy or sorrow
on his face. It was an old face, etched
with the lines of time and scored with a
lifetime's wisdom. In his eyes there were
glimmerings, flickerings, mysterious lights

that echoed the silver of his hair and
beard: gold, like the gold of a sunrise yet
to come, red, like the fire that had
consumed the ship, blue, like the sea
seared by the lightning's flash …

In his eyes there was a story yet untold.
It stirred angrily within him as he
watched the dying ship.

He wore a robe, dark, rich and heavy.
The garment swayed, a strange, rhythmic
movement of deep folds like secret
caverns ripe with mysteries: fear, hope,
knowledge, all were woven deep within
its fabric, for there was magic in the web
of it.

In his hand the old man held a staff, a
gnarled wooden stick. Yet it was more,

much more. It waited in his hand, as though it rested, as though no more than thought, no more than an eyelid's wink would fire its length with secret power. At his side there lay a book, red-bound and heavy, its pages worn with use, thumbed, scored, and learned, for they were pages saturated with the secrets of the enchanter's art.

The enchanter sighed, and turned towards the girl, whose pleading voice had broken through the dream that held him silent, watching.

'If by your art, my dearest father, you have put the wild waters in this roar, calm them,' his daughter begged. 'Poor souls, they perished ... '

Her father placed a calming hand against her cheek. 'Tell your piteous heart there's no harm done.' He looked towards the bay. The ship was gone. The winds were quieting. It had begun.

He drew his cloak about him, close, and held the staff before his face. He closed his eyes. And from the earth, the sky, the winds, he felt the powers flowing anew.

It had begun.

He turned towards his daughter. 'It is time.' He said it quietly, but with such force that instantly the girl grew quiet. 'I should inform you further,' he went on. 'Lend me your hand, and pluck my magic garments from me.'

Obediently the young girl grasped the

robe and eased it from her father's shoulders. She laid it to one side.

'Lie there, my art,' her father murmured. He took her by the shoulders, led her to a rock, and bid her sit on it. 'Wipe your eyes: have comfort.'

Wonderingly she did so. Trustingly she waited. And so the enchanter began the tale that wrote its bitterness behind his eyes. This wreck that she had seen was conjured by his magic art. The storm was no more than a magician's fancy, drawn from sky and sea by Prospero, the enchanter. She stared in dread: was her beloved father a man who killed for fancy?

But no, his voice calmed her: no man was lost from that burned ship; every one

still lived, as healthy as before the storm
had caught them. Every man believed
he had miraculously survived while all
the others drowned. Yet, truly, not a
single hair of any head was even wet.
Prospero nodded with pride. Now was
the beginning …

It was also the end. Twelve years of
preparation, in which every bone and
sinew, every thought, hope, desire was
sharpened to this moment. Twelve
years now drawing to a close. The hour
had come when he must tell Miranda
why. It had begun a long time ago, in
events long past, before ever they had
come to dwell here on this island. Did
she remember?

She had stirrings of faint memory, things far off but dream-like, the scattered remnants of a picture in a baby's mind: images of many women once attending her.

Prospero nodded. 'Twelve years ago, Miranda, your father was the Duke of Milan and a prince of power.'

Miranda frowned. 'Sir, are you not my father?'

Prospero gazed with eyes of love upon his innocent daughter. What would she make of the tale he had to tell; could her loving spirit understand such evil? His face grew dark with memories: trust betrayed, love turned sour; greed, ambition, murder …

Twelve years ago, he, Prospero, was
Duke of Milan, ruler of the most
powerful of all the states. Gentle
Miranda, his daughter, was no more
than a child of three, a princess. Duke
Prospero of Milan had a brother,
Antonio. In all the world Prospero loved
no one as he loved Miranda and Antonio.
He had trusted Antonio, as one could
trust a beloved brother.

Prospero was a man of learning.
More and more each day he grew
fascinated by his studies, drawn deep into
his books. Each day his library absorbed
him more than the affairs of state and
he left Antonio to rule the land for him.
Antonio learned to revel in the control

of men. There came a time when he no longer wanted just to act as duke, holding the keys of power in trust for Prospero. He yearned to be the duke, to wield that power, absolute power, for himself instead.

So the trusted brother Antonio, rotten with ambition, plotted with the King of Naples, a man long jealous of Milan's great wealth and power. One treacherous midnight, Antonio threw wide the city gates and let the enemy in. For this betrayal, the conquering King of Naples made Antonio Duke of Milan in Prospero's place.

Yet Antonio did not dare to kill his brother openly. By night he smuggled

Prospero to the coast. With tiny Miranda, he cast him to the sea aboard a rotten carcass of a boat to let the pitiless waters do what Antonio dare not.

But they survived, through Prospero's strength and unexpected kindness from one man among the enemy, Gonzalo, who took pity on their plight and gave them food and water. Knowing how Prospero loved his books, he smuggled some of the most prized volumes to the boat.

'Here in this island we arrived ...' Prospero rose, and lifted the magic robe about his shoulders. He had returned to his beginning: the storm, the wreck.

Miranda waited. What reason could her father have for these?

Prospero smiled, and though to Miranda it was her father's gentle smile, yet there was nothing gentle in it. It told again of twelve long years of preparation for this moment; twelve long years to perfect his enchanter's arts. Now fortune smiled on him and brought his enemies to the shore of Prospero's island. The king on board that tormented ship was Alonso, King of Naples – who had overthrown a rightful duke and placed his vicious brother on the throne. That prince was none other than the King of Naples' son. There was the king's brother, too, Sebastian. Above all, there was Antonio, the man who stole a brother's dukedom and threw him and his child into the waves to die.

Prospero raised a hand to stop Miranda's cry. 'Here cease more questions.' He placed his hand upon her head, 'You are inclined to sleep.' Beneath the magician's spell, Miranda's eyes grew heavy, and obediently she slept.

Now Prospero stood alone. One hand held his robe outstretched, the other held the staff high in the wind. He lifted his face towards the sky, and closed his eyes.

'Come away, servant, come. I am ready now. Approach, my Ariel, come,' he sent the call out from his mind.

There was a shimmer through the air and swiftly his servant came, a thing of glancing light, of movements quick as sight, of sounds like murmuring brooks.

'All hail, great master! Hail! I come to answer thy best pleasure: be it to fly, to swim, to dive into the fire, to ride on the curled clouds ...'

Eagerly the master greeted him. Had the tempest been performed exactly as he asked; was every instruction followed?

Eagerly the servant-spirit answered: flying as flames, he had blazed along the boat, brought lightning, thunderclaps, the mountainous waves, till all on board were mad with terror and all except the sailors plunged into the sea to escape the fires. First had been the king's son, Ferdinand, crying, 'Hell is empty, and all the devils are here!'

And yet – the master-stroke – they were all safe, all dry on land, not a single hair was damaged, garments glossier than before. They were scattered in groups across the island, each certain that all others must be dead.

All had been done by Ariel exactly as Prospero demanded.

The king's son, Ferdinand, was brought ashore alone. He was now lodged in a deserted corner of the island, plunged in deep melancholy, mourning the loss of father, friends and ship alike. The sailors were all safely stowed aboard the ship. It nestled (with no trace of fire) in a sheltered corner of the bay, hidden by curtaining mists. Below her decks the

sailors slept a deep, charmed sleep.

Prospero sighed. All faithfully done. 'But there's more work,' he spoke urgently.

Yet Ariel was restless. Prospero had promised freedom when this day's work was done. Twelve years Ariel had served the enchanter faithfully against that promise.

But now the reminder angered Prospero. 'Do you forget from what a torment I did free you?' he thundered. 'Have you forgotten the foul witch Sycorax?'

And Ariel trembled. Sycorax, once ruler of this island, had shut him painfully in a pine tree for refusing to obey her foul commands. There he had writhed for twelve agonising years.

'It was my art that made the pine gape wide and let you out!' Prospero's call to loyalty hung, threatening, in the air. And now the air grew still, for Ariel was silent.

Then, 'I thank thee, master,' came the whisper on the breeze. 'I will obey commands, and do my spiriting gently.'

'Do so,' the sorcerer's voice grew gentle too. 'And after two days I will discharge you. Go now. Transform yourself into a nymph of the sea.'

The spirit flew, and Prospero woke Miranda. There was still more to do, more he had planned. 'We'll visit Caliban, my slave,' he told her, and hurried her towards a hovel crouching, dark and evil-smelling, below a jutting rock.

'What, ho! Slave! Caliban! You earth, you! Speak!' his voice rang out. 'Come forth, I say!' Prospero grew angry.

A misshapen figure stumbled into view. The mouth drew back on snarling teeth, reddened eyes burned at his tormenter, for Caliban hated Prospero with a ravenous passion. Yet he feared him more, for any disobedience to the enchanter's will was swiftly punished with jabbing pains to torture every bone and sinew of his twisted body.

'This island's mine, by Sycorax my mother,' he hissed. 'When you came

first, you stroked me and made much
of me and then I showed you all
the qualities of the isle, the fresh
springs, the barren place and fertile.'
He fixed a haunted eye on Prospero.
'Cursed be I that did so! All the charms
of Sycorax, toads, beetles, bats, light
on you! You taught me language, and
my profit on it is, I know how to curse
you!'

And the creature that had once been
lord of all the island, waited,
sullen, to take his orders from
the enchanter.

For Prospero had need of Caliban, just
as he needed the spirit Ariel …

There was the lilt of music, the whirr of Ariel upon the breeze, a song that floated in the air and caught the listener and drew him on.

'Come unto these yellow sands ...' the spirit sang.

The listener followed, stumbling to keep pace, losing and finding the sounds again, drawn on, ever on towards the enchanter's cave.

It was Prince Ferdinand, the King of Naples's son, a fine gentleman, tall, young and strong, richly-dressed and handsome, though his eager face was shadowed with his sorrows. He had been sitting on a bank mourning his father's death when strange music had crept by upon the waters and snaked into his mind.

'Sure it waits upon some god of the island,' the young man breathed. There – the sounds again, floating about his head, now to this side, now the other …

Full fathom five thy father lies;
Of his bones are coral made;
Those are pearls that were his eyes …'

sang Ariel.

In awe the young man stopped. This could be no earthly sound, no sound from human voice!

Miranda, seated as her father placed her, saw the young man enter the clearing before their cave and leapt to her feet. In her young life she had seen only her father's long white beard and wrinkled face and the twisted form of Caliban. 'What is it?' she gasped to Prospero. 'A spirit? It is a spirit!'

'No,' Prospero smiled at her. 'It eats and sleeps and has such senses as we have. This gallant was in the wreck. He has lost his fellows and strays about to find them.'

Miranda feasted her eyes on the figure. She drank in the sight. Surely a god!

She was captured, and Prospero was pleased. All was as he desired, all as he planned. Secret thanks he sent to invisible Ariel hovering near, 'Spirit, fine spirit! I'll free you within two days for this!'

Ferdinand was a much-travelled young
prince, used to the rich beauties who
graced the royal courts of Europe. Yet this
vision of a windblown girl caught in a
sunlit glade, fixed him in wonderment to
the spot. Never had he seen such beauty!
It glowed like the sun itself. Surely this
must be the goddess of the isle, she who
conjured enchanted music from the air!

But then the goddess spoke, told
him she was nothing but a girl, and
miraculously, he understood the words!
In relief Prince Ferdinand tumbled out
the story of the wreck and all hands lost
with it, his father's death, who he was,
who else was on the ship, of Antonio,
Duke of Milan ...

At his usurping brother's name, pangs
of anger filled Prospero like the hot pains
he cast on Caliban. But there was much
else to be done, before the end. First (his
prime design) his powers must be used on
Ferdinand, all for Miranda. Love already
flowed between these two: every look
between them spoke of it. For this he had
drawn Ferdinand to the isle. But love
could be misplaced, and love could be
betrayed, and Prospero's life was testimony
to this. Before Ferdinand could win
Miranda as a wife, his love must stand the
test of strength and constancy and truth
and honesty. Love must be fought for.

And so he set the prince a task to prove
his worth – and a trial to test his

daughter's constancy. 'Come!' he ordered
Ferdinand. 'I'll chain your neck and feet
together: seawater you shall drink; your
food shall be the fresh-brook muscles,
withered roots and husks in which the
acorn cradled. Follow!' and he gave his
face a look more terrible than he had
shown before.

It did not frighten Ferdinand. The
more Miranda pleaded for Ferdinand
with all her heart, the more Prospero
frowned with stern, unbending harshness.
Yet the young prince bore his trials
bravely, declared that he could bear all
lightly if he could see the sweet face of
Miranda just once a day!

'It works,' breathed Prospero. And then

to Ariel, he promised through his mind,
'You shall be as free as mountain winds:
but then exactly do all points of my
command.'

'To the syllable,' came Ariel's windblown music ...

In a sunlit glade they gathered, a king,
nobles, lords, all saved from watery
death, all gorgeously attired in silks,
brocades and velvets unstained by salt-sea
wave. One old man, a wizened counsellor
to the King of Naples, was hopeful. They
were not dead: a miracle!

But Alonso, King of Naples, was
plunged in misery. His son was dead – he
had a vision of him wound grotesquely

with seaweed on the ocean bed …

'Weigh our sorrow with our comfort,' the old counsellor, Gonzalo, urged. In fact, he was that same Gonzalo who saved Prospero and Miranda from certain death twelve years before.

'Peace!' Alonso begged him.

'He receives comfort like cold porridge,' observed Alonso's brother, Sebastian, nastily. For Sebastian there were no comforts here, between wilting kings and counsellors who chattered like ancient parrots. But old Gonzalo gazed at the green, lush, sunlit place, drew the soft winds deep into his lungs, and thought dreamily of the world that might be built in such a paradise: no riches, no poverty,

all men equal, all women too, all
innocent and pure; no sovereignty ...

'Yet he would be king of it,' sneered
Sebastian, who thought a world without
riches to be seized would be a poor,
boring world indeed.

Prospero had heard enough: he sent
Ariel among them to float unseen and
fill the glade with mournful music, dark
tones to fill their eyes with heaviness,
drag down their limbs, till one by one
they slept.

Not all of them. There was another
scene in Prospero's drama shortly to
be acted: Sebastian and Antonio
remained awake.

To a discerning eye, these two could

not be easily told apart. Antonio was a
brother turned a thief, betrayer of a
brother's trust. Sebastian was brother to a
king, shortly to betray a brother's trust,
for he was a cold, ambitious man. Here
they were, marooned on a deserted island
beyond reach of any court or palace, far
from the powers of Naples or Milan.
Here, where they had secured neither
food nor drink nor shelter, nor any
means of getting off the island (ignorant
of the ship still hidden in the mists)
where life might rest upon one man's
help to another, these two remained true
to their own natures: they saw only one
means of advancement, even in the
sunshine of an island basking in the sea.

First Antonio and then Sebastian, quickly convinced by his faster-thinking fellow, cast their eyes on their companions, fast asleep, and on a weak-kneed king and dream-filled counsellor. Swiftly they concluded that if both were killed (Prince Ferdinand being already dead) why then Sebastian could be King of Naples, and Antonio rise to power with him. Two swift murders – and the power would be theirs.

From afar the enchanter heard. Again the games of power played with life and death as toys! But this time Gonzalo, once his friend would be the loser. In no more than the blinking of an eye, Ariel was sent to wake Gonzalo and the king.

Caught with drawn swords and guilty

faces, Sebastian and Antonio muttered of bellowing bulls (or was it roaring lions) against which they drew their weapons.

A glitter fired the enchanter's eyes. All as he remembered, all as he designed.

Caliban toiled along the beach beneath the load of wood, cursing, spitting, moaning with every grunting movement. Hatred for his master drove him like a furnace. His brain ached with memories of years of torment under Prospero. Spirits conjured – now like biting apes, now like hissing snakes – a thousand agonies from pricks and pinches, pains and cramps.

He stopped. A figure came towards him: jingling cap and tattered, flapping colours. It chattered, stumbled, mumbled, cowered, trembled, shook a bony fist towards the sky. To Caliban, all figures were but spirits sent by Prospero to torture him. In terror he fell to the ground and flung his tattered cloak across his head, in vain hope he would be invisible.

The figure was another bewildered survivor from the shipwreck that never happened: Trinculo, ageing jester to the King of Naples, miraculously alive, but facing, he believed, imminent destruction from freshly brewing storms.

More thunder, distant, rumbling

closer, ominous. Trinculo winced and clutched his arms about his skinny shoulders, running.

He saw the bundle on the ground and lurched to a halt. He pushed it cautiously with one toe. Dead or alive? A fish: it smelt like a fish, a very ancient fish-like smell …

A roll of thunder made the ageing jester jump. Weighing the stench of a fish-like dead-or-alive creature against the terrors of lightning that burned a ship to cinders, he chose the fish, and with his bony nose pinched tight against the stench, he crept under the hairy cloak.

Caliban felt the nearness of a torturing

spirit sent by Prospero and lay rigid, playing dead.

Towards this four-legged, four-armed hairy bundle on the beach, there came another apparition, one that swayed and tripped, hiccupped, swigged from a bottle, and lurched on. Stephano, the King of Naples' butler, floated to land on a wine barrel, had been filling his bloated stomach ever since. Now he stumbled across the hairy, smelly bundle. He gave it a hefty kick, reeled with the effort, burped and flopped with a gurgling squelch into the sand.

Whereupon Caliban howled, dreading some new and horrible torture from the spirits.

The drunken butler pushed his bleared eyes close to the stinking bundle. A four-armed, four-legged howling creature! Some island monster in a fever? Stephano lurched to a sitting position. An island monster, cured and tamed, might yet be taken back to Naples. What a present for an emperor! Stephano raised his bottle to the threatening clouds and drank to the idea, then prodded the monster.

Caliban groaned. 'Do not torment me. I'll bring my wood home faster,' he begged beneath the cloak.

'He's in a fit now,' announced Stephano. 'He shall taste of my bottle.' He nodded sagely, for the bottle was cure

for any ill. He stuck it in the monster's
mouth, and leapt in shock to find
it was a monster of such skill that it
could suddenly, upon drinking, produce
two voices, one in the top end (where a
man might expect to hear a voice) and
one in the bottom end that, when filled
up with wine, miracles of miracles, called
him by his own name!

Being a brave man, he pulled at
the monster's smaller legs and discovered
his good friend Trinculo. At which the
two friends danced for joy, comparing
notes on escape from watery graves.

Caliban was feeling a warm inner
glow that seemed uncannily connected
to that bottle. Wonderingly he gazed

at it and the portly man in tattered
breeches who nursed the magic potion.

'Have you not dropped from heaven?'
he asked.

'Out of the moon, I do assure you,'
chortled Stephano.

It was enough for Caliban: this was a
god with potions that could lift a man
from earth and make him fly. He fell to
his knees before his god. 'I'll show you
every fertile inch of the island: I will kiss
your foot,' he pledged, and did so. 'I'll
show you the best springs, I'll pluck you
berries, I'll fish for you ...' And in his
overflowing love he offered the god all
the riches of this kingdom, as once he
had to Prospero.

'A most ridiculous monster, to make a wonder of a poor drunkard,' observed Trinculo the jester, blinking.

'Lead the way,' cried Stephano. 'Trinculo, the king and all our company being drowned, we will inherit here. This will be our kingdom! Bear my bottle,' he said to Caliban, majestically, and Caliban took the bottle as though it were a delicate jewel nestling on a gilded cushion, and held it up aloft, and led them, singing …

'Ban, Ban Cacaliban,
Has a new master: get a new man …
Freedom, hey-day! Hey-day, freedom!'

To test Miranda in her love for Ferdinand, Prospero had set him Caliban's work. Did handsome youths in gorgeous clothes, transformed to filth and sweat and rags, still shine for her? Or did Ferdinand at dirty work become a Caliban in her young eyes? Ferdinand toiled at fetching and carrying logs, thousand upon thousand. Being a king's son and unfitted for work of any kind, he struggled beneath the burden. Miranda wept to see him so: she offered to do it for him; she shared his misery. But he was valiant: driven on by Miranda's wistful adoration, he manfully endured his trials.

Prospero was satisfied. Their love was not destroyed by harshness; it grew bolder. Ferdinand swore he prized and honoured Miranda above all else, and Miranda answered with love. Prospero almost wept with joy. Before this day was over, Miranda would be Ferdinand's wife – the future Queen of Naples. Soon this act of Prospero's drama could be closed.

Stephano was playing king, and passed the bottle. Caliban drank, adored his god, and passed the bottle. Trinculo drank, jeered at Caliban, and passed the bottle. Caliban told them of his master who had by sorcery seized the island.

'From me he got it,' Caliban cried, and stared through desperate eyes at god Stephano. 'If you will revenge it on him, you shall be lord of it and I'll serve you!'

Planted in Stephano's brain, the idea was good. Decorated here and there with something of the customs of this master, and something of his possessions, and something of his pretty daughter, the idea was even better.

'Monster, I will kill this man: his daughter and I will be king and queen, and Trinculo and yourself shall be viceroys.'

They shook hands on it, and passed the bottle, and Stephano sang the song again that he had been teaching Caliban.

'Flout 'em and scout 'em,
And scout 'em, and flout 'em;
Thought is free.'

To their consternation the tune was
changing! Lilting pipes drowned out their
merry verse, and though they struggled to
hold a course, the ghostly music
overwhelmed and terrified them.

'Are you afraid?' asked Caliban
curiously. 'Be not afraid. The isle is full of
noises, sounds and sweet airs, that give
delight and hurt not.' A dreaming peace
had come upon the creature as he spoke;
as though he melted once again into this
island that was his.

'This will prove a brave kingdom to me,
where I shall have my music for nothing,'

Stephano yelled, and gathered more
courage from the bottle.

'When Prospero is destroyed,' Caliban
reminded him.

'The sound is going away,' cried
Trinculo, bolder for the reminder of their
paradise to come. 'Let's follow it and
after do our work!'

'Lead, monster,' Stephano waved
Caliban on, 'we'll follow …'

But Ariel, musician of the air, had
heard their plot, and swift as a salt-sea
breeze across the bay had carried news to
Prospero: Caliban the slave had found a
god with a faded, jingling henchman by
his side, and these three lurched towards
him, bent on murder for the kingdom of

the island. Again the game of power was played, with life and death as toys.

With aching limbs and heavy heart, the King of Naples sank to rest. Even the sea mocked their search for the king's son, Ferdinand. All the lords and nobles faltered, too – even Gonzalo was beyond cheerful words; his old bones ached too much with tramping. Sebastian and Antonio, though, hovered close, preparing for their plot. As soon as opportunity was there (Sebastian nodded to Antonio). Tonight, Antonio urged Sebastian.

Their secret dialogue broke off: strange, solemn sounds, like deep murmurs, were rising from the earth. They moved nervously together. The air grew misty. They huddled closer. From the gleaming centre of the mists came twisting shapes – half animal, half human, grotesque and ugly. Yet they smiled, bore a banquet to the centre of the glade, table upon table piled with food, and then with nods and bows they melted back into air and only the echo of the music floated on.

But they had left the feast. King and lords stared round nervously. King and lords awaited further happenings. The glade was quiet. The lords were hungry – hungrier by the minute. Sebastian was all for eating. Alonso drew back anxiously.

They moved towards the laden
tables cautiously.

There was a clap of thunder and
lightning seared across the glade. A great
bird swooped between them, a monstrous
giant with hag-like human face and the
body of a taloned vulture. The vast
wings smote the table and instantly the
banquet vanished.

'You are three men of sin,' the
apparition cried. The thundering voice
was agony in their ears. 'On this island
where man doth not inhabit, you
amongst men being most unfit to live,
I have made you mad!'

Sebastian and Antonio drew swords.

'You fools!' the terrible voice rang out.

58

'I and my fellows are ministers of Fate:
your swords may as well wound the loud
winds, or kill the waters, as diminish one
feather in my plume!'

The voice rose to the rumbling of an
earthquake, trees and rocks shook
with its wrath. 'But remember—' The
warning shivered in the air. 'Remember!
You three did supplant good Prospero
from Milan: for which foul deed, the
powers have incensed the seas and
shores, yes, all the creatures, against your
peace. They have bereft thee, Alonso
of thy son, and by me they do pronounce
a lingering torture, worse than any
death, shall step by step attend you
and your ways.'

There was a roll of thunder, so
deafening and the light so blinding,
that they hid their heads. And
when they looked again, the bird
had gone.

In his wake soft music played to mock
them, the shimmering spirits of the air
returned, and before their helpless eyes
and hands, taunting, the spirits danced
and carried out the table.

The glade was empty now, filled only
with their terror.

Invisible above, Prospero, waited.
Now let the terror work. Now let their
agony of fear bore madness deep within
each villainous heart ...

The time had come for Prospero to free Ferdinand. Being so close now to the end, the enchanter wished to give one final gift to these young people, to reveal the wonders of his powers, before the end, to them.

He closed his eyes, and through his mind he sent the call: 'Spirits, which by my art I now call up,' he cried, and rejoiced as his many spirits thronged about the united couple. They danced in celebration of the lovers: spirits of all the island's secret places, of the woods and trees, the streams and lapping seas, of hill and valley, sky and earth …

Then he froze. A thought, ice cold, had shot into his brain. In the warmth of the young people's love he had forgotten Caliban and the conspiracy against his life. With that memory, warm visions of love and plenty he had conjured up were gone. Ferdinand and Miranda stared in dismay at Prospero, grown dark with bitterness again.

Prospero moved swiftly to comfort them.

'Be cheerful. Our revels now are ended. These, our actors, were all spirits and are melted into air! We are such stuff as dreams are made of, and our little life is rounded with a sleep ...'

But Caliban was coming. Summoning Ariel, Prospero gave commands. Light as

the sea-blown breeze, the spirit-servant
flew and returned. In his arms rich
garments gleamed with all the colours of
the rainbow. Prospero had charmed a
storm, a wreck, a spirit-feast, to confuse
and madden a treacherous king and
villainous lords; he had brought forth a
spirits' dance of blessing for young lovers.
Now, to thwart the drunken murderers,
he chose the vanity of gaudy clothes to
deck a would-be king …

They were not so jovial as before,
Stephano, Caliban and
Trinculo. Ghostly music had led
them on a stumbling dance through
thorns and briars, and now their bottle

63

lay beneath the rancid scum of some
filthy gurgling pond. Trinculo whined,
Stephano bellowed, and Caliban was
terrified that Prospero would hear them.

But Trinculo saw the clothes. With a cry
of ecstasy he fell upon them. Garments
for a king, finery for a king's minister,
riches beyond a jester's dreams!

'Let it alone, you fool,' hissed Caliban.
'It is trash.'

But already a battle royal raged
between a would-be king and a
would-be minister: cavorting, squabbling,
flourishing, snatching, heads, arms, legs,
thrusting in and out of sleeves and
tearing necklines.

'I will have none of it,' yelled Caliban,

'we shall lose our time, and all be turned to barnacles or apes!'

But it was neither apes nor barnacles for them. Blood-curdling yowls, the snapping jaws of ravenously baying hunting dogs erupted from the forest, and before the snarling terror of those phantom beasts, the would-be killers fled.

Prospero and Ariel watched their quarry run. 'At this hour lie at my mercy all mine enemies,' triumphant Prospero spoke. 'Shortly shall all my labours end. And you, Ariel, shall have the air at freedom: for a little, follow, and do me service …'

The spirit bowed his head; the final act was drawing near – and after, liberty.

'Now does my project gather to a head: my charms crack not – my spirits obey.' Prospero stood ready. Round his shoulders swayed his magic robe. By his side stood Ariel. 'How's the day?' Prospero murmured to his faithful spirit servant.

'On the sixth hour; at which time, you said our work should cease.'

'I did say so, when first I raised the tempest.'

Since then: a king and treacherous brothers had been maddened with their guilt and fear, imprisoned at his will, locked fast by charms.

The final power. His they were, for

life or death. The final choice now lay before him.

'Your charm so strongly works on them, that if you now beheld them, your affections would become tender,' Ariel's music reached into his mind. He stood quietly. 'Do you think so, spirit?' he asked.

'Mine would, sir, were I human,' the spirit answered.

Silence grew about the enchanter and his tender servant-spirit. The final choice must now be made. But Prospero was listening to Ariel's music.

Finally he spoke. 'Go release them, Ariel,' the enchanter said. 'My charms I'll break, their senses I'll restore, and they shall be themselves.'

Joyfully, Ariel sped away. Prospero stood alone. He closed his eyes, and spread his arms out wide so that the robe swirled, rich with magic powers. 'I have bedimmed the noontide sun, called forth the mutinous winds, and between the green sea and the blue vault of the sky I have set roaring war: to the dread rattling thunder have I given fire ... and by the roots plucked up the pine and cedar ... graves, at my command have waked their sleepers, opened and let them forth ...'

But here would be the end. He knew that now. Here, when the final act was over.

He drew a magic circle, and into it they came, the maddened king, the staring brothers, the bewildered lords, held in

Prospero's enchantment, silent, asleep, awaiting the final vengeance.

Now they must see him as he was, when all began: as Prospero, one-time Duke of Milan. Swiftly, singing, for his liberty was nearing and he danced with joy, Ariel helped the old man to remove the robes of Prospero the enchanter. Now he stood as Prospero, the Duke.

Slowly, with no violence, Prospero released his victims from their sleep.

They stared in disbelief: Prospero, long believed dead, come back from the grave! Their minds, a few moments ago twisting in crazed terror, calm and clear again! There followed a scene of such bewilderment and awe, recognitions,

explanations, grief, remorse, apologies
and reconciliation, as the island had
never seen before, nor would it ever
again. Alonso, King of Naples, who had
long felt an inward torture for the deeds
committed twelve long years ago, wept for
sorrow at his villainy and begged
forgiveness. Gonzalo was in ecstasies of
joy, relief and amazement all in one.

Antonio and Sebastian, who in a trice
had understood that Prospero knew all
and could, with but a single word, betray
their villainy to Alonso, now faced the
ultimate of judges: their own consciences,
newly-sharpened by the terrors of this
island magic.

From them all, Prospero had one

demand: the restoration of his dukedom, lands, wealth and rights.

Alonso, of course, still mourned the loss of Ferdinand: Prospero drew back the curtains of his cave and revealed Miranda. Quietly, and needing nothing more, she played at chess with none other than Prince Ferdinand. More wonderment, embracing, joy, and explanations.

Miranda stared in rapture at the glorious array of gilded lords. 'How beauteous mankind is!' she cried. 'Oh brave new world, that has such people in it!'

'It is new to you,' said Prospero, with a lifetime's weary knowledge.

They still mourned the loss of sailors,

captain, ship. One by one they were
produced, lifted through the balmy air
and placed before them by invisible Ariel.

'Was it well done?' whispered Ariel
to Prospero.

'Bravely,' whispered Prospero to Ariel.
'You shall be free. Set Caliban and his
companions free; untie the spell.'

And so to the final revelation: the
hapless trio stumbled in, limply hung
with stolen clothes, cowed and sheepish
now. Caliban, expecting vicious
punishment, found in Prospero a new
master, decked in unknown finery, and
generous in forgiveness. Instantly he
transferred his adoration to this better
master, and wondered how he had

ever adored a drunkard as a god.

So now, instead of vengeance, hospitality was all that Prospero offered. On the morrow they would embark for Naples to see the marriage of Ferdinand and Miranda – the final bond of reconciliation tied. Then Prospero would turn for home – for Milan.

'I promise you calm seas, auspicious gales,' the enchanter murmured. And in his mind he called for the last time to Ariel. 'My Ariel, chick, that is your charge: then to the elements be free ...'

There was a flutter in the breeze as of a dragonfly's wings, and with a whisper of farewell and love to Prospero, the spirit flew to liberty.

Prospero stood alone, high on the rocky headland. Ariel and Caliban were free: one to the winds, and one to his island paradise.

Prospero had planned his magic all for vengeance: yet in the final hour it had brought him face to face with tenderness and charity. In the magic circle drawn for punishment, he had seen his victims' misery was no less terrible than his own twelve years before, his ruthless use of power no better than the abuse he had suffered at their hands. That was the final music Ariel had played for him.

So now the sea would take his magic and bury it deep. First his robe, and then his book, and finally his staff, broken in

two, he cast into the waves. For that brief moment, as he saw them flying from his hands, there was unutterable despair. He was a man again, no more than a man. Gone was the magic that had given him power over earth, air, fire, water, life and death, and over an infinity of dreams.

But after the despair came a new peace: as a man he had the power of choice, of knowledge, understanding, compassion, pity, love. And in that there was untold richness, glory, hope – and dreams.